The Cutest Critter

story by **Marion Dane Bauer**   photography by **Stan Tekiela**

Adventure Publications, Inc.
Cambridge, MN

Dedication
For Terry Berggren, who makes awfully cute critters.
   —Marion Dane Bauer

To my daughter Abby, who loves baby animals as much as I do.
May your love of nature grow with each passing year.
   —Stan Tekiela

Rose-breasted Grosbeak egg photo by Carrol Henderson

Cover design by Jonathan Norberg
Book design by Lora Westberg

10 9 8 7 6 5 4 3 2 1

Copyright 2010 by Marion Dane Bauer and Stan Tekiela
Published by Adventure Publications, Inc.
820 Cleveland St. S
Cambridge, MN 55008
1-800-678-7006
www.adventurepublications.net

ISBN-13: 978-1-59193-253-6
ISBN-10: 1-59193-253-X

The Cutest Critter

Who's the cutest critter in the land?

Is it a bear cub sleeping?

Or a fawn just learning to stand?

Is it a foal playing peek?

Or a baby bird with wide-open beak?

Maybe it's a fox kit in black mitts.

Or perhaps this pair of opposites.

Baby raccoons in a struggle?

Or lynx kittens having a snuggle.

Is it a wolf pup collecting a kiss?

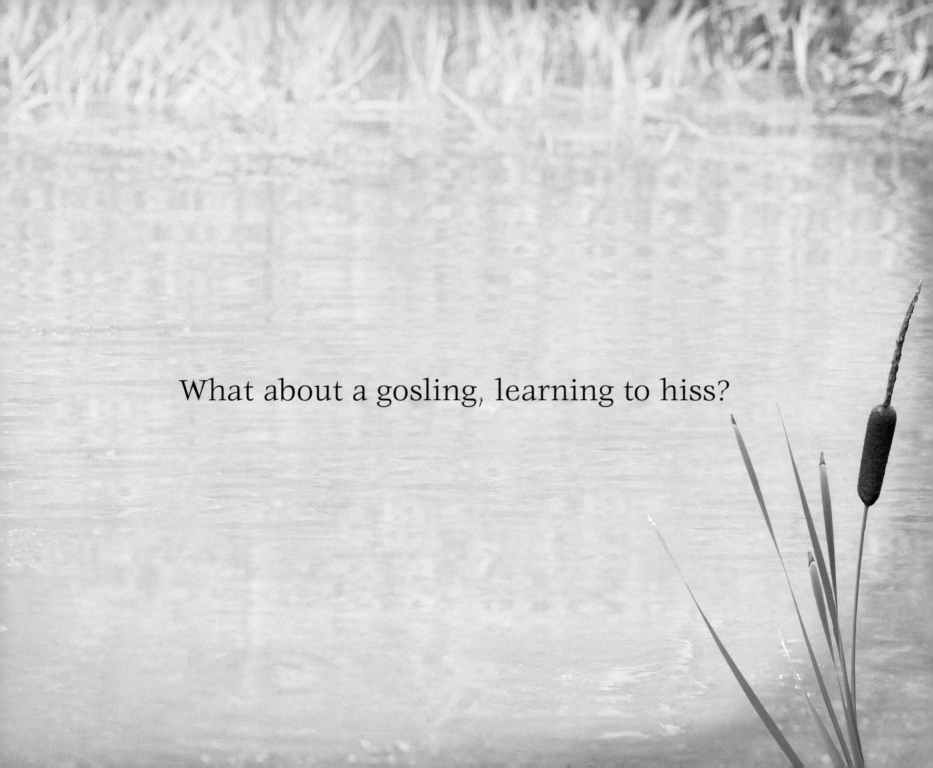

What about a gosling, learning to hiss?

Then there's this bison calf getting a drink.

Or a baby skunk working up a stink.

Babies are cute. That's certainly true.

But I've searched this world, through and through,

and of all the young critters I ever knew

not a single one is cuter than you!

Black Bear

Baby Name: Cub

Cute Factor: Bear cubs are born with short, fine fur, and they look a lot like teddy bears. They need their moms to keep them warm, so they are extra cuddly.

Born to Be Wild: Bears grow very quickly. In fact, when they stand on their hind legs, they're bigger than a person. They have strong, sharp claws, which they use to dig into trees while searching for insects to eat.

White-tailed Deer

Baby Name: Fawn

Cute Factor: Fawns look just like that cute forest friend Bambi. Their soft, tan fur with white spots helps them hide on the forest floor during bright spring days.

Born to Be Wild: Adult deer are fast runners. They use their hard hooves to scrape the ground while looking for food. Male deer grow sharp antlers, which they use for fighting with other male deer.

Wild Horse

Baby Name: Foal

Cute Factor: Foals have long, skinny legs that make them look a little silly, but they can walk within minutes of birth. Their legs may look wobbly, but foals can run, prance and jump quite well.

Born to Be Wild: Adult horses have muscular legs, which help them run very fast. When in danger, horses kick with their back legs to hurt or scare away other animals.

Rose-breasted Grosbeak

Baby Name: Chick

Cute Factor: Grosbeak chicks hatch without many feathers, so they don't really look like birds. Although they look a little scrawny, they sure are cute, sitting in their nests, begging for food with their mouths wide open.

Born to Be Wild: Adult grosbeaks are known for their large bills, which they use to crush seeds before eating them. Male grosbeaks have a rose triangle on their chests while the females are streaked brown and white to blend with their surroundings.

Red Fox

Baby Name: Kit

Cute Factor: Another cuddly looking creature, fox kits are famous for their sweet expressions and brown eyes. Their pointy ears seem far too big for their faces.

Born to Be Wild: Foxes use their ears to listen for nearby animals. They can run up to 30 miles per hour, about the speed of a car driving through town. Foxes can jump and pounce like a cat.

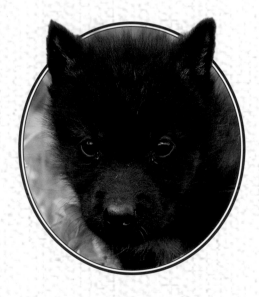

Gray Wolf

Baby Name: Pup

Cute Factor: Baby wolves are chubby and playful, like household puppies. They come in many colors, not just gray. They can even be black or white. Pups love to wrestle with their brothers and sisters.

Born to Be Wild: Wolves live in families or packs. Working together, they hunt larger animals, such a deer. They have sharp teeth and some of the most powerful jaws in the animal kingdom.

Northern Raccoon

Baby Name: Kit

Cute Factor: Who is that masked bandit? It's a baby raccoon. Kits look like tiny adults, and they make soft, tender sounds when they are happy.

Born to Be Wild: Adult raccoons are quite smart. They use their human-like hands to climb trees and to catch crayfish underwater. Raccoons even pry open garbage cans, looking for food.

Canada Lynx

Baby Name: Kitten

Cute Factor: Baby lynx look like cuddly, household kittens. They have blue eyes, pointy ears and fluffy paws that seem too big for their bodies.

Born to Be Wild: Lynx grow up to become skilled hunters. They have long, sharp claws, and their large paws help them walk in deep snow and over rough surfaces.

Canada Goose

Baby Name: Gosling

Cute Factor: Newly hatched goslings look a little like a plastic bathtub toy, except fuzzy. They are covered in a thick coat of yellow feathers, which helps them float.

Born to Be Wild: Adult geese are very protective parents. They hiss at anything that gets too close to their babies. They also use their strong wings to swat away intruders.

American Bison

Baby Name: Calf

Cute Factor: Much like a baby cow, bison calves have big, chocolate-brown eyes and long, black eyelashes.

Born to Be Wild: Adult bison are very large and surprisingly dangerous. They can weigh as much as four baby elephants, and they can run as fast as a fox. When threatened, they will charge. People who think they are slow, lazy and tame can be in for a surprise!

Striped Skunk

Baby Name: Kit

Cute Factor: Baby skunks look like tiny, cuddly versions of their moms and dads, but there's no need to plug your nose. These furry critters can't spray their stinky spray until they are eight days old.

Born to Be Wild: After eight to ten days, look out. Young skunks can aim and spray their famous, foul-smelling, oily substance at targets up to fifteen feet away. Their stinky smell is their main defense and keeps most other animals away.

About the Author

Marion Dane Bauer is the author of more than sixty books for young people, ranging from novelty and picture books to early readers, both fiction and nonfiction, books on writing, and middle-grade and young-adult novels. She has won numerous awards, including the Minnesota Book Award, a Jane Addams Peace Association Award for her novel *Rain of Fire*, an American Library Association Newbery Honor Award for her novel *On My Honor* and the Kerlan Award from the University of Minnesota for the body of her work. She is a writing teacher and was first Faculty Chair for the country's first Master of Fine Arts in Writing for Children and Young Adults program at Vermont College of Fine Arts. She continues on as faculty there. Her writing book, the American Library Association Notable *What's Your Story? A Young Person's Guide to Writing Fiction*, is used by writers of all ages. Adults who are interested in writing for children have found it especially useful. Her books have been translated into more than a dozen different languages. For more about Marion and her books, visit her website at www.mariondanebauer.com.

About the Photographer

Stan Tekiela is a naturalist, author and wildlife photographer with a Bachelor of Science degree in Natural History from the University of Minnesota. He has been a professional naturalist for more than 20 years and is a member of the Minnesota Naturalists' Association, Outdoor Writers Association of America, North American Nature Photography Association and Canon Professional Services. Stan actively studies and photographs wildlife throughout the United States. He has received various national and regional awards for outdoor education and writing. His syndicated nature column appears in more than 20 cities and his wildlife programs are broadcast on a number of Midwest radio stations. Stan has authored more than 100 field guides, nature appreciation books and wildlife audio CDs for nearly every state in the nation, presenting many species of birds, mammals, reptiles and amphibians, trees, wildflowers and cacti.

Stan resides in Victoria, Minnesota, with his wife, Katherine, and daughter, Abigail. He can be contacted via his website at www.naturesmart.com.

Get the First Two Children's Books from the Award-Winning Duo

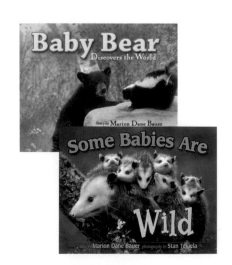

If you enjoyed *The Cutest Critter,* you'll love these other titles that pair Marion Dane Bauer's touching stories with Stan Tekiela's incredible photography:

Baby Bear Discovers the World
Follow along as Baby Bear ventures into the forest to meet other animals. This popular book won the 2007 Mom's Choice Award for Most Outstanding Children's Book.

Some Babies Are Wild
A 2008 Mom's Choice Award winner, *Some Babies Are Wild* highlights the most precious of relationships: the unbreakable bond between mother and child.